Weekly Reader Books Presents

Hattie Be Quiet, Hattie Be Good

by Dick Gackenbach

An EARLY I CAN READ Book®

Harper & Row, Publishers
New York, Hagerstown, San Francisco, London

To Ann Marie

This book is a presentation of Weekly Reader Books. Weekly Reader Books offers book clubs for children from preschool through high school. For further information write to: **Weekly Reader Books,** 4343 Equity Drive, Columbus, Ohio 43228.

Published by arrangement with Harper & Row, Publishers, Inc. Weekly Reader is a federally registered trademark of Field Publications. I Can Read Book is a registered trademark of Harper & Row, Publishers, Inc.

Hattie Be Quiet, Hattie Be Good
Copyright © 1977 by Dick Gackenbach

Library of Congress Cataloging in Publication Data
Gackenbach, Dick
    Hattie be quiet, Hattie be good.

    (An Early I can read book)
    SUMMARY: Hattie's helpfulness is unappreciated
by her mother and her sick friend, Shirley Rabbitfoot.
    [1. Rabbits—Fiction.   2. Short stories]
I. Title.
PZ7.G117Has3   [E]   76-58697
ISBN 0-06-021951-3
ISBN 0-06-021952-1 lib. bdg.

Something Nice From Hattie

"I think I will

do something nice

for my mother today,"

said Hattie.

"I will make her
a special breakfast
with eggs and peanut butter!"
But Hattie
could not find
the frying pan.
She could not reach
the top of the stove.

"I will clean the house
for Mother instead,"
Hattie said.

She went to the closet
to get the vacuum cleaner.
It was too heavy.
Hattie got tangled
in the cord.

Hattie decided,

"Cleaning is too hard for me!"

Then Hattie remembered

something her mother

was *always* asking

her to do.

"Hattie," her mother always said.

"Please sit down

and be quiet

for an hour."

"That is it!" shouted Hattie.

"That is the nice thing

I will do for her."

6

So Hattie sat in a big chair
and was very quiet.
The clock in the corner
went *tick-tock*, *tick-tock*.
It was nine o'clock.

Hattie heard her friends

playing outside.

But she did not

make a sound,

not even a whistle.

Mother saw Hattie

sitting quietly in the chair.

She asked,

"What is wrong with you?"

"Nothing," said Hattie.

Mother felt her head.

"No fever," she said.

"But something is wrong.

You are too quiet.

I will make you

some hot soup."

Hattie stayed
in the chair.
She twisted.
She squirmed.
She held her
breath until
her eyes popped.

She wished to be anywhere
but in that chair.
Finally, the clock struck ten.
The hour was over.
"HOORAY," Hattie shouted.

She ran up the stairs

and slid down the banister.

WHACK! CRASH! BANG!

Hattie landed

in the umbrella stand.

Her mother

ran from the kitchen

to see what made the noise.

"Oh, thank goodness,

you are feeling better,"

she said.

"And now,

will you please

sit down and be quiet

for an hour."

"Oh, no!"

said Hattie.

"I just *did* that!"

Get Well, Shirley Rabbitfoot

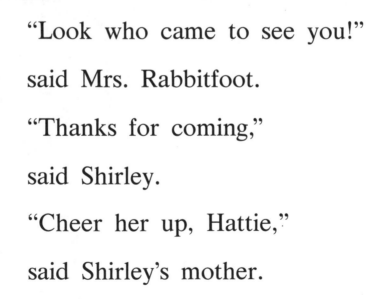

"Look who came to see you!"

said Mrs. Rabbitfoot.

"Thanks for coming,"

said Shirley.

"Cheer her up, Hattie,"

said Shirley's mother.

16

"I will wait downstairs

for the doctor."

"Okay," said Hattie.

Hattie looked at Shirley.

"Boy, do you look terrible,"

she said.

"You need pillows
under your feet."
"What for?" asked Shirley.
"To make the blood
go to your head.
Then your color will
come back."

Hattie shoved

three pillows

under Shirley's feet.

"How is that?" she asked.

"Awful," said Shirley.

"Now I will
wash your face,"
said Hattie.

"Germs love dirt."

"I am not dirty,"
yelled Shirley.

But Hattie

washed her face anyway.

"Agh-h-h," screamed Shirley.

"You got soap in my eyes!"

Shirley wiped her eyes

and put the pillows back.

Mrs. Rabbitfoot

returned with Doctor Hare.

Doctor Hare took

Shirley's temperature.

"Hm-m-m," said Doctor Hare.

22

"Let me see your tongue,
Shirley."

Shirley stuck out her tongue.

"Hm-m-m," said Doctor Hare.

"It is just a sore throat.

A day in bed and some ice cream

are what you need.

I will be back tomorrow,"

he said.

"And I will go
and get the ice cream,"
said Mrs. Rabbitfoot.
Hattie asked Shirley,
"What flavor ice cream
do you have here?"

"Chocolate Almond Delight!"

said Shirley.

"Move over,"

said Hattie.

"Now what are you doing?"

asked Shirley.

"Feel my head,"

said Hattie.

"It is burning up."

"It feels cool to me,"

said Shirley.

"See my tongue,"

said Hattie.

"It has white spots."

"It looks red to me!"

said Shirley.

28

"Oh-h-h,"

moaned Hattie,

"my poor throat."

"Baloney," said Shirley.

Hattie was still groaning
when Mrs. Rabbitfoot
returned with the ice cream.
"There is some
for Hattie too,"
she said.
"What for?"
said Shirley.
"She is not sick.
She is a big phony."
"But she did come visit you,"
said Mrs. Rabbitfoot.

"Yes, I cheered you up,"

Hattie reminded Shirley.

"Well, okay," said Shirley.

"She can have some ice cream."

"WOW," said Hattie.

"There is only one thing

I like better than

Chocolate Almond Delight!"

"What is that?" asked Shirley.

"My friend

Shirley Rabbitfoot,"

said Hattie.